D0971635

Caroling in the snow.

The English Roses

Hooray for the Holidays!

CALLAWAY ARTS & ENTERTAINMENT

19 FULTON STREET, FIFTH FLOOR, NEW YORK, NEW YORK 10038

PUFFIN BOOKS

Published by the Penguin Group
Penguin Young Readers Group, 345 Hudson Street, New York, New York 10014, U.S.A.
Penguin Group (Canada), 90 Eglinton Avenue East, Suite 700, Toronto, Ontario,
Canada M4P2Y3 (a division of Pearson Penguin Canada Inc.)

Penguin Books Ltd., Registered Offices: 80 Strand, London WC2R 0RL, England

First published in the United States of America by Callaway Arts & Entertainment and Puffin Books, 2008

1 3 5 7 9 10 8 6 4 2

First Edition

Produced by Callaway Arts & Entertainment
Nicholas Callaway, President and Publisher
Cathy Ferrara, Managing Editor and Production Director
Toshiya Masuda, Art Director • Nelson Gómez, Director of Digital Technology
Joya Rajadhyaksha, Editor • Amy Cloud, Editor
Ivan Wong, Jr. and José Rodríguez, Production
Jennifer Caffrey, Publishing Assistant

Special thanks to Doug Whiteman and Mariann Donato.

Callaway Arts & Entertainment, its Callaway logotype, and Callaway Editions, Inc., are trademarks.

Fluffernutter is a registered trademark of Durkee-Mower, Inc. and is used by permission. All rights reserved.

Library of Congress Cataloging-in-Publication Data is available.

Puffin Books ISBN 978-0-14-241124-7

Printed in the United States of America

www.madonna.com   www.callaway.com   www.penguin.com/youngreaders

All of Madonna's proceeds from this book will be donated to
Raising Malawi (www.raisingmalawi.org), an orphan-care initiative.

The English Roses

by **Madonna**

With Amy Cloud

Hooray for the Holidays!

PUFFIN
CALLAWAY

New York
2008

illustrated by Jeffrey Fulvimari

→ Book 7 ←

Contents

CHAPTER I

Daydream Believer

i love the ballet!!!

The English Roses.

Those three words really shouldn't need further explanation at this point. I mean, unless you've spent the last few years climbing to the top of Mount Everest, or sailing the Black Sea, or exploring the Amazon, you have no reasonable excuse!

Those three words should be as familiar to you as some other choice three-word phrases: No she didn't! Keep it real! Do it up! But, anyway, if you *did* happen to spend the last nine hundred days or so stranded at the top of Everest or floating about the Black Sea and you need some enlightenment, your hookup is here! For those three words—the English Roses—refer to the five most fab young lasses in London. Their names are as follows: Charlotte Ginsberg, Amy Brook, Grace Harrison, Binah Rossi, and Nicole Rissman. And get ready, because they are about to rock your world!

900 days doing one of the following:

✓ MT. everest ✓ the black sea ✓ the amazon

Our story begins on a blustery day in mid-December. A bitter wind scuttled the last of autumn's leaves along the city sidewalks. Though the sky was heavy with gloomy clouds, no snow had yet fallen in London.

Stuck inside Mrs. Moss's sixth-grade classroom, Charlotte Ginsberg was daydreaming.

Not the kind of gentle mind wandering that you can just—BAM!—snap back into reality from, either. No, this wasn't a simple, "whatever shall I wear tomorrow?" type of fancy. This was a full-blown trance . . . a trance that just happened to involve Charlotte and a deep emerald flowy skirt that draped just so, flaring out above her knees. (*You* know the kind I'm talking about!) In her fantasy, Charlotte was Clara, the star performer in her

favorite ballet, *The Nutcracker*, lost in a world of fairies and dancing flowers. As a troupe of evil mice arched in attack, she was whisked deftly to safety on the arm of her valiant nutcracker prince. The two glided across the stage in perfect harmony; and as the prince swept her up in a flawless *pas de deux*, her ears rang with thundering applause from the audience. Charlotte held her head high, gazing into the clear blue eyes of her tender-hearted prince . . . eyes that looked vaguely familiar, sort of similar to . . . yes, almost exactly like . . .

The boy who was at this very moment jabbing his pencil into the back of her crisp white blouse!

Jolted from her dream, Charlotte whirled around in a fury. "William!" she hissed. "Do you MIND?"

"What, Charlie?" William smiled innocently. "Just wanted to make sure you were paying attention to Mrs. Moss's lesson about cell division. This is important stuff, Charlie. I wouldn't want you to miss it."

Charlotte twisted her mouth to hide the tiny grin playing on her lips. For the star of Charlotte's daydream also happened to be the most insufferable boy on the planet—or, at the very least, at Hampstead School—William Worthington! He was forever torturing Charlotte in Mrs. Moss's class. And ever since the two had played leading

roles in the sixth-grade production of *Romeo and Juliet*, Charlotte found that William snuck into her daydreams far more often than she might have liked. For, as irritating as he could be, William was TA: totes adorbs (which translates to "totally adorable." Duh!).

Oh yes, I should probably mention now that Charlotte was on an abbreviation kick, constantly peppering her statements with "abbrevs," as she preferred to call them. The English Roses were used to Charlotte's phrases *du jour*, as she seemed to have a new one every couple of months. The abbrevs, however, had become something of a small problem, as anyone speaking to Charlotte had to periodically stop her mid-conversation for translation.

As Charlotte opened her mouth to spit back a witty retort, she felt something prickly on her ear. It wasn't a pesky itch, or a mote of dust, or a stray hair tickling her. It was that creepy feeling you get when you know someone's staring at you. You *are* familiar with that feeling, aren't you? It's *très* eerie! Well, Charlotte could feel a pair of eyes burrowing holes into the side of her head like field mice in a meadow. She glanced to her right and saw that those eyes belonged to Jeanette Jones. As soon as she saw Charlotte looking, however, Jeanette bent down and began taking notes furiously.

Jeanette Jones wasn't someone to whom Charlotte usually gave any particular amount of thought; and if she was your classmate, I bet you wouldn't, either. She wasn't especially pretty, or

popular, or smart. She was a decent student but hardly ever spoke in class, and spent most of recess quietly sitting by herself or dangling motion- less from the monkey bars. Jeanette was the kind of girl who always seemed to laugh a bit too loudly when someone made a lame joke; she was always chosen last for teams in gym class. The English Roses

had always thought she was a little bit . . . well, odd
would be the word. Rumors circulated that she
lived in an old, ramshackle town house filled with
chickens and pigs, and to conserve water was only
allowed one shower per week. Once, Carole James
claimed she heard Jeanette talking to herself when
she thought no one was around. And her fashion
sense definitely left something to be desired. Her
pants always seemed to be too short or too baggy,
and her skirts never fit properly. Instead of ribbons,
Jeanette tied her two braids with bits of colorful

yarn. Charlotte always was nice to her at school but otherwise tried to steer clear. Because, the sad truth of things was, sixth grade was hard enough without a social outcast dragging you down.

But before she had time to think anymore about it, she heard a familiar THWACK! The sound of Mrs. Moss's omnipresent ruler hitting her desk cracked through the air like a clap of thunder.

"Attention, please, class!" she barked. "I have a brief announcement to make before we continue our preparation for national merit exams."

CHAPTER 2

Secret Santa!

this is charlotte's hand ←

Charlotte could almost feel the class collectively rolling their eyes. Besides "detention" and "quiet down," Mrs. Moss's favorite words were "national merit exams." She constantly nagged the class about preparing for these tests, whose actual significance was a mystery to her students.

Mrs. Moss's voice softened considerably as she removed her wiry spectacles and sat down on her desk. A heavy sigh escaped her chest. "Now, in the spirit of the season, I have decided—at Miss Fluffernutter's suggestion, mind you—that we shall have a Secret Santa gift swap. Harold will be coming around with a hat, and you will all draw exactly one slip of paper. You shall purchase a gift for the person whose name is written on that slip. There is to be absolutely no trading of names. There is a ten-pound limit on gifts that shall not be exceeded under any circumstances. Next Monday we will open our gifts at a festive holiday celebration."

The class seemed to draw a breath of astonishment as excited whispers filled the air. Mrs. Moss was known for her strict attendance policies and adherence to the official Hampstead School Code of Conduct, but she was not renowned for her jovial spirit. That honor went to Miss Fluffernutter, the English Roses' much-cherished fifth-grade teacher, who was also a trusted friend. Vivacious and fun, Miss Fluffernutter was always doing about a million things to help others yet was always happy to lend an ear or a hand or a thoughtful word. That's just the kind of person she was.

Charlotte gave the English Roses a quick thumbs-up. A Secret Santa gift exchange seemed almost TGTBT (that's "too good to be true")!

"Yo-yo-yo, Charlie, I'm sayin' this right, so don't

be chillin', pick a name from my hat and you know you'll be illin'.'" Harold Fieldbinder was a skinny boy with an unfortunate case of postnasal drip who fancied himself the school's master MC.

Charlotte dipped her hand in the hat and fished around until her fingers grasped a piece of folded paper. She opened it. The name inside read: "Evelyn Eaves."

Charlotte looked over at Evelyn Eaves, who, as usual, was surrounded by a cluster of fawning boys. If Jeanette Jones was the sixth grade's quiet mouse, Evelyn was definitely its queen bee. She carried herself in a way that seemed to scream, "I don't care what anyone thinks of me," and she dressed like a fashion model. Today, for instance, she was wearing a fitted, high-waisted, Kelly

green skirt cut right above the knee with a white puffed-sleeve blouse. Her shiny brown hair was pulled into a high ponytail that swung about when she laughed. Evelyn Eaves was most definitely something special—and Charlotte knew that her Secret Santa gift had to be simply perfect!

The bell chose that moment to ring loud and

clear, a cry of freedom if there ever was one. The class gathered their things for lunch. As Charlotte was collecting her one-of-a-kind Louis Vuitton lunch case from her schoolbag, she felt a tap on her shoulder.

"Wil-liam, honestly . . ." she began, but turned to find that instead of William Worthington she was staring right into the eyes of Jeanette Jones.

Jeanette looked up at Charlotte shyly. Her mouth was filled with a chunk of her mousy brown hair, which she chewed on thoughtfully. Charlotte was revolted, then immediately felt hot with guilt. After all, Jeanette might have been strange, but she had never done anything bad to Charlotte.

"Hi, Charlotte," Jeanette stammered softly. "I . . . really like your shoes."

I really
like
your
shoes

"Uh, thanks," Charlotte replied. "They were a Hanukkah present from my sister."

Jeanette paused, as if she wanted to say something else, but instead turned and ran down the hall.

CHAPTER 3

Holidays on Ice

don't you just LOVE this time of year?

The English Roses sat down for lunch at their usual round table at the far-east corner of the cafeteria. It was deemed the MDS (that's "most desirable spot"), as it provided both lots of privacy and shelter from the watchful gaze of their most un-favorite lunch lady, whom Nicole (the writer of the group) had

nicknamed Hally Tosis (she *did* have extremely offensive breath!).

Amy poked at her leftovers (Amy's family almost always had takeout since her mum just had a baby, her stepdad was a banker, and neither had time to cook) and sniffed as Charlotte took out her lunch— foie gras and crisps, with sliced pineapple on the side. She made one of her famous, supremely grotesque faces, shaking her head of fabulous red curls. "Nast! Charlie, your lunch definitely has an eww factor of ten."

Charlotte spread the light brown pâté on a crisp

and crunched it happily. "Nigella's foie gras is simply divine, Aim!" she said. Nigella was Charlotte's cook. Charlotte's family was, as some would say, rolling in dough. Besides a cook, the Ginsberg family had a butler, a housekeeper, and even a driver!

The other girls giggled. "What exactly is 'fois gras' again?" asked Grace squeamishly.

"Technically speaking, mashed duck liver," Nicole informed them.

"Nicole, do you actually memorize the dictionary each night?" Amy giggled.

amy got

Candy darling

Nicole looked slightly embar-rassed. "Well, I have spent time reading it before. When I don't have anything else to read, that is . . ."

Binah smiled and put her arm around Nicole. "Well, that's what we love about you, Nikki! You're like our very stylish, witty, walk-ing dictionary." Nicole grinned. Sometimes Charlotte thought of Binah as the glue holding the five best friends together.

Amy put down her fork with a bang. "Okay, girls. Let's talk Secret Santa! I got Candy Darling." Candy Darling was a cool chica whom the Roses sometimes invited to their sleepover parties. She and her twin sister, Bunny Love, were incredible dancers.

grace got:
Carole James.

NICOLE got HAROLD

(ick)

Grace looked annoyed as she plunked her paper slip down on the lunch table. "Well, I have Carole James, crybaby extraordinaire." It was true; Carole James did seem to tear up at any available opportunity, a skill that often proved useful, especially when she got into trouble. Grace, however, had no patience for such antics.

"I got Harold." Nicole winced. "Ick."

"Well, at least he'll be easy to buy for," Amy suggested. "A large gold medallion, a new microphone, or anything to advance his hip-hop career should be appropriate."

The girls giggled. "I got Ben!" Binah said happily, and all the girls nodded and sighed in approval.

BINAH got

BEN

Ben was Binah's special boy friend. Not "boyfriend"—no, Binah wasn't ready to place that particular label on their friendship. But Ben did make Binah's heart beat a little faster, and he and Binah had a special understanding.

"And I," Charlotte said finally, "have as my Secret Santa"—she paused dramatically, studying her perfect manicure (FYI, her fave nail polish shade is Ballet Slippers) and glanced around the table expectantly. The girls leaned in slightly.

"Evelyn Eaves."

There was a stunned silence.

"Wow," Amy said finally. "Evelyn's the most stylish girl in school!"

"What are you going to get her, Charlie?" Grace asked.

It's the most wonderful time of the year!

"I'm not sure yet," Charlotte said thoughtfully. "Something fabulous!"

"But there's a ten-pound price limit!" Nicole reminded them. "Mrs. Moss said so."

"We don't have to stick to that," Charlotte scoffed. "At least, I'm not. I mean, what kind of gift can you really buy for ten pounds? Certainly not one that could be classified as fabulous!"

The girls didn't know how to answer that one. But they didn't have much time to consider it, either, as the air was suddenly filled with the sound of happy humming. It grew louder and louder, until it was right behind them.

"Jingle bell, jingle bell, jingle bell rock, dah-da-dee-DAH and doo-dee-dee-DOO," sang Miss Fluffernutter happily.

"Hi, Miss Fluffernutter!" chorused the English Roses.

"Why, hello girls! Happy holidays to you all!" Clutching a handful of disorganized papers dotted with colorful scribbles, Miss Fluffernutter quickly hugged each girl—not an easy thing to do when your arms are full, but she never could resist giving a hug. Tall and wiry, with her mass of frizzy curls wrangled into two disheveled pigtails, she was wearing a green pleated skirt, red-and-white striped tights, and matching red velvet flats with gold buckles. Earrings shaped like gold bells rang in her ears when she shook

her head back and forth. Compared to
the drab skirts and boring pants suits
Mrs. Moss wore, Miss Fluffernutter's clothes were
like a breath of fresh air.

"I just love your tights," Binah told her approvingly.

"Oh, do you?" asked Miss Fluffernutter, staring
down at her candy cane–striped legs. "They may
make my legs look like a barbershop sign, but I just
couldn't resist them. I do love the holidays so!"

3 impish santas

The girls grinned happily. Miss Fluffernutter was a ray of warm sunshine on such a blustery December day.

"I hope you're all enjoying your lunch. I had to gobble mine quickly today since I'm such a busy, busy bee. Papers to grade, and, of course, I'm not even close to being done with my holiday shopping yet. There never seems to be enough time; December just skates by!" she gushed. "Oh, speaking of skate, are you all coming to the Holidays on Ice ice-skating party on Wednesday night? Remember, all proceeds will benefit my charity, the Helping Hands. Bring your family! It's such a lovely cause, and ice-skating is one of my favorite wintertime activities. Don't you just love—"

"Of course, Miss Fluffernutter." Nicole

gestured around the table. "We'll all be there."

"Oh, that's simply marvy! Wait a minute, is that Harold I see over there? He's going to be helping me DJ. I'd better skedaddle! Ta-ta, girls!" And with that she was off, a flustering whirlwind of frizz.

"OMG!" Grace said. "I almost forgot about Holidays on Ice! I wanted my brothers to come, but I think they have practice that day." Grace's twin older brothers, Michael and Matthew, were in high school.

"Oh, rats!" Amy said, her face falling. "I was going to ask Michael to skate with me."

Michael   Matthew

"You totes wanna TMB, Aims," Grace teased.

"TMB?" Nicole asked, perplexed.

"'Touch my brother,'" Grace explained. "It's a new abbrev!"

Charlotte nodded her head in approval, but inside her stomach flip-flopped. She was excited about the party, but the idea of skating with boys made her a wee bit nervous.

The conversation then turned to the skating party, appropriate outfits ("CIB," Amy advised. "Casual is better. I mean, we aren't figure skaters!"), and, of course, the couples skate.

Binah looked just as nervous as Charlotte felt. "So," she said softly, "what do you do when you skate with a boy? I've-I've never done it before."

"Oh, it's no biggie." Amy jostled her curls. "I've

done it lots of times. Basically you just hold hands and skate around in a circle while they play a romantic song and make the lights all dim and woozy."

Charlotte thought it sounded terrifying. Binah looked as if she felt the same. Grace scoffed. "No thanks. I don't want to risk being injured skating around with some dumb boy. I've got a big game coming up!"

"You're just saying that because Anthony is out of town!" Nicole teased. Anthony Strong was a cutie and an amazing football player. (Note: "football" is to Brits what "soccer" is to Americans.)

Anthony strong!!!

Though Grace wouldn't admit it, she had a bit of a soft spot for Mr. Strong.

"Well," Nicole said, "I'm probably going to be in the snack bar all night, studying for finals. I'm bringing my laptop."

Charlotte wished she could hide behind a laptop, too. She wondered what William Worthington thought of couples skate. Sure, he teased her a lot in class, and they had shared a clumsy kiss in the play—but that was the theater! And—as Charlotte well knew—anything goes in the theater!

Just then, Jeanette Jones doddered through the cafeteria. She usually ate by herself, so Charlotte

was surprised when she stopped at the English Roses' table.

"Hi, Charlotte." She smiled shyly, pulling a tattered book out of her bag. "I just finished reading this, and it was so good! I thought you might like to borrow it?"

"Umm, sure," Charlotte said hesitantly.

"Hi, Jeanette!" Binah jumped up. "How are you? Your hair looks really cute!"

"Thanks, Binah." Jeanette beamed.

The bell rang; and as she walked back to class with her friends, Charlotte wondered why Jeanette kept trying to talk to her today.

CHAPTER 4

Sisterly Advice

em ma

"Later, girl," Charlotte waved good-bye to Grace as she started up the semicircular path to her front door.

"Bye!" Grace called, bumping a football against her head as she continued down the street. As far as football went, Grace had game. She was the star player on the Hampstead girls

team, and she liked to boast that she could usually out-ball the boys.

Charlotte lightly crunched the soft blanket of snow that had covered the circular driveway. Her feet snug in furry UGGs, she pretended she was an Eskimo princess making the slow and arduous trek

back to her homeland. *Just a few more seconds until we reach safety*, she assured herself as she climbed the steep steps that led to her front door.

Once inside, she pulled off her puffy coat with the fur-trimmed hood. Winston, the family butler, appeared, as usual, with a cup of hot cocoa on a tray. "Something to warm you, Miss?" he inquired as she stepped out of her boots.

"Oh, thank you, Winston," she said sweetly, accepting the hot treat. Winston always made the best cocoa. "Is my mother here?"

It was rare that Charlotte's mum was around, especially near the holidays. She was always off running some charity drive or planning an event or getting her picture taken for the socialite section of the newspaper. Sometimes, Charlotte wished she had a normal mum, who stayed home and made hot cocoa herself. But then she felt guilty for even having those thoughts. Her family had so much, and many out there had next to nothing. Take Binah, for instance. Her mother died when she was very little, and her father was always out working hard to make ends meet. Binah ended up having to do most of the chores and cooking herself, and money was always tight at her house. Charlotte knew she should be grateful that her own family had such an excess of riches.

"Ma'am is out at the moment," Winston said, then paused. He looked as if he wanted to say more, but instead he turned and shuffled back toward the kitchen.

Charlotte's
MUM
→

Just as well, Charlotte thought. She went upstairs to her room and placed her leather bag neatly on her favorite pink velvet chair, which had once belonged to her grandmother. Homework beckoned, but pangs of loneliness tugged at her heart. With all the events of the day swirling about her head, Charlotte needed to talk to someone!

Maybe Emma's home, she thought excitedly. Emma was Charlotte's cooler-than-thou older sister. Beautiful, smart, sweet, and popular, Emma was a star ballerina with a drop-dead gorgeous boyfriend named Oliver who was captain of their school's football team. Charlotte's greatest hope was that someday she'd be just like Emma.

Charlotte tiptoed up to Emma's closed door and pressed her ear against the shiny, varnished wood.

Emma's voice echoed from within. "Oh no HE DID NOT!" she shrieked, her voice cascading into giggles. Obviously the girl was on a VIC (very important call). But Charlotte really needed to talk to someone, and since her mother wasn't around . . .

"Em?" the door creaked as she eased it open. "Can I talk to you for a sec?"

"Hold on," Emma said. "Gwen, can I call you back in a few? Amaze." She threw her pink cell phone down on the bed and gestured to Charlotte. "What's up, dork?"

Charlotte smiled. "Dork" was her sister's affectionate name for her. "Well, it's nothing, really. I mean, not a huge deal. It's just that our class's Secret Santa is coming up, and we drew names today."

Emma slapped her forehead in astonishment. "Oh, my coolness! Sixth-grade Secret Santa! I can't believe Old Mossy"—this was what Emma and her friends called Mrs. Moss—"is letting you guys do something fun! She never did that with us."

"I know," Charlotte agreed, nodding her head. "It's so weird. I think Miss Fluffernutter is rubbing off on her."

"Must be. I mean, we always said her name might be Moss, but her heart is made of ice." Emma shuddered at the memory. "So . . . who'd you get?"

miss Moss!
ICY heart

"Well, that's the problem," Charlotte continued. "I got Evelyn Eaves! She's, like, the queen bee of the sixth grade."

Emma nodded her head in appreciation. "So there's pressure," she concluded.

"Totally! I mean, I just have to get her something super-fabuloso, you know?" Charlotte gushed. "Mrs. Moss says there's a ten-pound spending limit, but I can't think of one single cool thing that would cost so little! And if I get her something lame, she'll laugh at me —or something worse!"

Emma shrugged. "Don't kill yourself, Charlie. Get her a lipstick."

"But is that enough?" Charlotte winced at the thought.

"Isn't it supposed to be the thought that counts?" Emma smiled, bending her knees in a perfect plié.

Charlotte swatted the air as if a fly was buzzing around her face. "Of course grown-ups say that," she said, "but no one really means it."

It was true. In fact, her mum always seemed to spout that wisdom right after Charlotte opened her yearly gift from their Auntie Harriet. Auntie Harriet was her mum's slightly wacky aunt who lived in Cornwall and was about one hundred years old, but for some reason she seemed to think that

Charlotte was still a toddler. Last year she had given her a Little Miss Muffett Beauty Set, which included fake lipstick and a plastic compact with a sticker of phony cheek stain in the center. When she had opened it, Charlotte and Emma had ROFL (that's "rolled on the floor laughing"), which had caused their mum to turn pink with anger and remind them that it was the thought that counts. But she could tell that even her mum was embarrassed that her aunt would give such a random gift.

"I just wouldn't worry too much about it," Emma said, studying an imaginary pimple in the mirror. "Everything changes in middle school anyway."

Charlotte hesitated. She looked at her sister, with her perfect dancer's body and gleaming black hair. Emma always had boys chasing after her, always won the lead in the school play, always got straight As without even trying. Why couldn't she be more like Emma?

"Emma, did you ever do couples skate?" she asked in a small voice.

Emma giggled. "OMG! Couples skate! I almost forgot about that. So cute!"

Charlotte was annoyed. She stared at her fingernails and gently pushed back a cuticle. "I'm not a five-year-old!" she reminded her crossly. "This is important, Emma. Do you think I should skate with a boy—I mean, if a boy asks me?"

Emma straightened her face. "Sorry," she said, flopping down on the bed next to Charlotte. "Sometimes I forget what it's like to be a sixth grader. Of course it's important. Very important! But you should only skate with someone if you want to—if you really like him and you're in the mood to skate around with him. If you're not ready, then don't do it."

Charlotte considered this advice. She didn't know if she was ready. The whole ordeal seemed all at once terrifying and exhilarating. The idea of holding William Worthington's hand for an entire slow song gave Charlotte a certain thrilling feeling in the pit of her tummy—sort of like when she was trying out for a big part in drama class.

CHAPTER 5

Queen Bees Can Sting

You know that when you're really nervous about something, the time leading up to the nerve-wracking event seems to fly by, don't you? At least, that's the way it always seems (no, it hasn't yet been scientifically proven). And the days leading up to the Holidays on Ice party seemed to speed by in

the bat of a (lightly mascara-ed) eyelash. Finally, it was the big night! Binah's father dropped off the English Roses at the front door of the ice rink.

"Bye, Papa," Binah called, kissing him on the cheek. "Royston will take us all home after the party's over."

As the girls were tumbling out of Mr. Rossi's pickup truck, they came upon the endearing sight of Miss Fluffernutter struggling to carry about twenty items, from ice skates to a brightly colored banner.

"Hello, girls!" she cheerfully bellowed, dropping a hot pink skate. "Whoops! Oh, hello there, Mr. Rossi!"

"Miss Fluffernutter!" Mr. Rossi called, and one could swear that his eyes grew a bit brighter at the sight of the frizzy-haired teacher. "Please, let me help you!"

Mr. Rossi quickly parked his truck, then rushed over and grabbed the wayward skate, and the girls helped Miss Fluffernutter carry her things in to the rink.

Once inside, Nicole rushed to the snack bar while Binah chatted with her father and Miss Fluffernutter, and Charlotte, Grace, and Amy sat down to put on their skates. The Student Activities Committee had completely transformed

the dingy old ice arena into a winter wonderland. Strings of icicle lights dangled from the ceiling, while red and green paper chains brightened the sidelines. Charlotte leaned over and laced up her skates as tightly as she could. Next to her, Amy winced. "Grace! You're tying them way too tight!"

"I'm just doing it for your own good," Grace said. "You don't want to be wobbling around out there." She emitted a low whistle. "Get a load of Evelyn Eaves!"

Evelyn breezed by wearing a flared, green velvet skating skirt. It reminded Charlotte a lot of the one she herself wore in her *Nutcracker* daydream from a few days earlier. Charlotte immediately felt dowdy in her jeans and sweater. And dowdy wasn't a feeling Charlotte was used to!

"I can't believe she's wearing a skirt that short!" Amy murmured. "It's totes inapprops!" (translation: totally inappropriate).

Amy and Grace skated off. Charlotte told them she needed to fix her skate, but truthfully she just wanted to search for William. She found him in a group with other boys, doing shoot the duck and similar show-offy moves on the ice. William caught her looking and

flourish #1

Totes inapprops!

winked. Charlotte's stomach flopped around in her belly. She was working up the courage to approach him when she felt a shadow hovering over her.

"Hi, Charlotte," Jeanette Jones said in a hesitant voice. "I just love your outfit!"

Charlotte, taken by surprise, wasn't sure what to say. "Oh, uh, hi." She glanced down at Jeanette's skates, which looked like the kind she had seen her own mother wearing in old photographs. They were aged and dirty, and were also obviously much too big for Jeanette, who could barely stand on the ice.

Jeanette saw Charlotte checking out her skates. "They used to be my sister's," she explained, wobbling back and forth. "They don't fit too well, but Mama said they had to do."

Charlotte nodded. "They're very . . . retro," she said finally. "Adorbs!"

Jeanette gave Charlotte an odd look, then after a moment chuckled in a way that made it clear she

très awks

Baby, it's cold outside!

had no idea what Charlotte was talking about. "Hee hee. Uh, yeah. Adorbs. That's exactly what I thought. Anyway, I don't know if I ever told you, but you were so good in the play this year! You really stole the show."

"Um, thanks," Charlotte said. She felt badly, but didn't know what to say to Jeanette. It was *très* awks.

"I was wondering," she began. "Maybe sometime you could come over? I like to write plays. We could even perform one together . . . if you want."

Charlotte, caught off guard, was speechless. She willed her mouth to open, but no words would come out. Go over to Jeanette's *house*? What was she supposed to say? What would people think if they saw?

Before she could dream up a response, someone whirled by Jeanette, bumping her from behind. Jeanette toppled over onto the ice. "Yow!" she shrieked.

There was a chorus of giggles from behind Jeanette as a flash of green whirled by. Evelyn Eaves smartly performed a perfect figure eight,

then skidded to a stop with a flourish. "Sorry," she smirked. "I must have slipped."

Jeanette rubbed her bum, then looked down, her face red with shame. Charlotte felt awful, but she didn't know what to do.

"Char-baby! Look at how adorable you are! Come with me, there's something I need to talk to you about," she said, grabbing Charlotte's arm.

And just at that moment, skating away with Evelyn, Charlotte looked back at Jeanette struggling to stand up on her too-big hand-me-down skates and hated herself a tiny bit. She hated herself for caring so much what others thought of her—for not jumping up to defend Jeanette like she knew she should do. Why did she want Evelyn to like her so much?

Evelyn whisked her to the snack bar and sat her down on a stool. "Want an ice cream? My treat!"

"Uh, sure," Charlotte said, smoothing her rumpled jeans. She craned her neck, looking for Jeanette, but couldn't find her.

"I just wanted to save you from having to talk to Jeanette." Evelyn gave Charlotte a knowing nudge. "You can thank me later."

"Um, actually," Charlotte began, "I wasn't—"

Grace, Amy, and Binah skated by. They waved at Charlotte and threw her puzzled looks.

"I mean, what a surprise, to look over at Char-baby, the most adorbs girl EVER, and see her talking to—"

(flourish) #2

Suddenly, the lights in the rink dimmed, and soft spotlights cast their glow over the ice. "Irreplaceable" by Beyoncé came on, and an army of boys appeared beside Evelyn.

"Hey, Evelyn, skate with me?!"

"No way, man, she promised me first skate!"

Evelyn shot them all looks of disdain. "Who are you going to ask to skate, Char?" She paused, then flashed a knowing smile. "You know, I saw William looking over at you earlier."

"Really?" Charlotte hoped the look on her face didn't seem too eager.

"Totally," Evelyn assured her. "You two are so cute together; I swear, I just wanna eat you both up."

This picture both alarmed and disturbed Charlotte.

"Do you want me to say something to him? I can totally ask him for you!"

"No!" The word burst out of Charlotte before she even had time to think about the question. "I mean, no thank you," she finished, pulling herself together. Charlotte never, *ever* forgot her manners. So much so, in fact, that the English Roses dubbed her Miss Manners.

"So, who do you think William has for Secret

Santa?" Evelyn asked, shooting Charlotte a playful look. "I heard it's a pretty, dark-haired girl!"

"Oh yeah?" Charlotte asked, in a way she hoped wouldn't seem too anxious. Charlotte was a dark-haired girl. The idea of William giving her a Secret Santa gift definitely gave her tummy tumbles.

"Yeah!" Evelyn said. "That's what I heard."

As Evelyn dashed off to skate with one of her many admirers, Charlotte gazed at the couples circling the rink. She was happy to see that Binah and Ben were out there, as was Amy with her Big Crush, Ryan Hudson (the dreamiest boy in school! as Amy always squealed). And, surprisingly, so was . . .

"Miss Fluffernutter?" Charlotte couldn't help but say her name out loud. For there was Miss

Fluffernutter hand in hand with Binah's father! And Charlotte had never seen Mr. Rossi so happy before. The little line of worry that she always thought was a permanent facial feature had somehow disappeared. He looked like a giddy little schoolboy, skating round the rink with a goofy grin plastered on his face.

Charlotte scanned the room for William, but she couldn't find him. Was he out skating with someone? Or in the bathroom? Or maybe he was fed up with the entire evening and had gone home? Charlotte

felt a pang of sickness in the pit of her stomach. She knew that Evelyn would have no problem asking William to skate. Neither would Emma. So what was wrong with her?

"Charlie!" Grace and Nicole plopped themselves on either side of Charlotte. "Did you hear about what happened to Jeanette?" Grace said breathlessly. "Evelyn Eaves knocked her down, apparently. I didn't see it happen, but Jeanette's face was bright red from crying, and her dad came and picked her up."

"Oh," Charlotte's voice belied the hollow feeling inside of her. She silently prayed that her friends didn't know she had anything to do with that situation.

"Speaking of Evelyn," Nicole questioned

suspiciously, "why were you hanging out with her just now?"

Charlotte felt nervous. "I'm not sure, really." She shrugged. "She came over and said she needed to talk to me about something. Then couples skate began, and she ran off with some bloke."

"That girl is just plain mean," Grace glowered. "What she did to Jeanette was unforgivable. Don't you think, Charlie?"

"It really sounds quite awful," Charlotte agreed. And it *was*. But was she supposed to not talk to Evelyn because of what Evelyn had done to Jeanette? And if Evelyn was so evil, why was she the queen of popularity?

CHAPTER 6

Secret Spender?

"Hey, Charlie!" Grace nudged her friend. "Which shade do you think Carole will like better? Truly Vamp or Petal Sweet?"

It was the Saturday following Holidays on Ice, and the English Roses were Secret Santa shopping

at Marks & Spencer. Grace held up two rose-colored nail polish shades for Charlotte to inspect because, as she put it, Grace didn't know her way around a makeup counter "to save her life."

"Hmm." Charlotte pondered the two tubes of glossy color. "For Carole, I think Petal. No, no, Vamp. Wait, no. I'm wrong. Carole would definitely look better in Petal."

Charlotte had to admit that she wasn't her usual self at the makeup counter that day; well, the week had been rather stressful, after all! The rest of the skating party had passed without further event—as it turned out, William had gone home early due to a bellyache. Apparently, he had eaten *all* of the RUNTS in the vending machine (or so he boasted to Charlotte in class the following day). Jeanette was absent that day. When she returned to school Friday, she was walking in a peculiar manner. While Charlotte was sharpening her pencil, Jeanette tried to show her the "wicked bruise" on her backside.

"It's all blue and purple, like a terrible thunderstorm cloud!" she gleefully exclaimed. "Don't you want to see it?"

Charlotte could think of nothing she'd rather see less. "Oh, that's okay, though I'm sure it's lovely," she quickly added, trying to be polite. "I'm just glad you're all right." But then Evelyn had come by and offered Charlotte a piece of candy. She made a big show of offering one to Jeanette, too; Charlotte suspected it was to make amends for the unfortunate ice-skating incident—and Charlotte scurried back to her seat.

So now it was Saturday, and Charlotte had to find a gift for Evelyn, but didn't see one single thing that was good enough.

Amy and Nicole rushed up to the counter. Nicole happily held up a bag from Music City. "I found a CD for Harold!" she said happily. "So, mission accomplished, and I don't even have to give him a gold medallion."

"Aren't these tights marvy?" Amy waved around a package of plaid dance wear. "Candy will look so cute dancing up a storm in these!"

"They're the cutest," Grace agreed. "Well, I'm buying Carole this nail polish. Charlie picked it, so I know the color will be just ri—YOW!!"

Binah had run up to Grace and poked her in the ribs. "Gotcha, Harrison!" She was breathless and looked flushed and happy. "I found the cutest thing for Ben's kinkajou at the pet store. And I also got Ernesta a new toy." Ernesta was Binah's adorable little pet gerbil. The girls ooh'ed and ahh'ed over Binah's purchases.

"Everyone's found their Secret Santa gift but me!" Charlotte wailed. "What am I going to do??" She could see the newspaper headlines now: YOUNG GIRL PERISHES FROM EMBARRASSMENT DUE TO LAME SECRET SANTA GIFT.

"Chill out, Charlie!" Grace soothed. "It's no big deal."

"It most certainly is a big deal," Charlotte said in a crabby tone. "Secret Santa is only two days away! I don't have much time left."

"If I were you," Amy said angrily, "I wouldn't get her anything. The nerve of that girl, pushing Jeanette!"

"Oh, Aim." Charlotte sighed. "I can't do that. Plus, she apologized. And she did offer Jeanette some candy the other day."

"Big whoop," Grace muttered. "Candy doesn't erase what she did."

"Well, all of this shopping made me totally famished, guys," Binah piped up, trying to smooth things over as usual. "Who wants some fish and chips?"

The Roses all agreed that some food would be the perfect finish to their afternoon shopping spree. The five girls linked arms and were walking out of

the store when a gleam caught Charlotte's eye. She turned and saw a woman at the jewelry counter holding up a simple, thin, gold-link chain on which hung a rectangular-shaped pendant made of a glass. A tiny diamond was suspended inside. Charlotte thought it was beautiful and elegant and every-thing a grown-up piece of jewelry should be. But more importantly, it was *sooo* Evelyn Eaves.

Charlotte dragged her friends over to the jewelry

counter and asked the saleslady to show her the necklace. "It's our last one," the saleslady breathed. "Perfectly exquisite, if I may say so."

Charlotte turned to her friends. "Don't you think this would be perfect for Evelyn?"

Grace wrinkled her nose at the lady's potent perfume, which she thought smelled a lot like the spray her father used when he'd spent too much time in the bathroom. "It looks expensive, Charlie," she snorted.

THaT'S IT !!!

"Shush, Gracie!" Charlotte hissed. "It really is lovely," she cooed. "How much?"

"Well, it's regularly priced at £89.99, but since it's today's Special Value item, I'm so very pleased to be able to give it to you at a bargain price of only £49.99," the saleslady replied eagerly.

Charlotte nodded. "That's quite a steal!" she gushed.

The English Roses looked at one another in bewilderment. Amy nudged Charlotte. "Um, but it's forty pounds over the spending limit," she whispered.

Charlotte looked annoyed. "So what? It's absolutely divine. I have my allowance and some savings. I can afford it," she argued.

"But why would you want to spend that kind of

money on *her?*" Grace asked in what Charlotte thought was an accusatory manner.

Charlotte was tired of feeling guilty. Was it a crime to try and find the perfect gift for someone? "Listen, it's none of your concern what I get Evelyn," she snapped. "And I can spend as much as I want to!"

Grace looked hurt. "Back *off*, sister." She grimaced, holding up her hand. "Just trying to help."

Charlotte forked over the cash and the smelly saleslady handed her a tissue-wrapped package.

A fishy tension affected the girls' lunch that day—and it wasn't because of the fish and chips! For, as much as she didn't want to admit it, Charlotte knew her friends didn't approve of her purchase. As they picked through their grub, the girls felt a gloomy cloud hang over their friendship. Maybe Secret Santa wasn't such a great idea after all!

CHAPTER 7

Miss Manners? Hardly!

The rest of the weekend passed without too much fanfare. Charlotte was excited to show her sister Evelyn's Secret Santa gift. But when she did . . .

"Wow! How much did you spend on this?" Emma gasped, fingering the delicate gold chain.

"Price doesn't matter!" Charlotte responded. "Isn't it fabulous?"

"Well, it's beautiful," she began. "But it's a little . . . much, isn't it?"

Charlotte felt embarrassed. "Do you think it will look like I'm trying too hard?" she worried.

"Nah," Emma said quickly, gently placing the necklace back into its velvet box. "It should be fine."

But Charlotte didn't feel fine.

She also couldn't keep a certain boy from entering her mind. No matter how much she tried to push him out, someone with the initials W. W. kept stubbornly intruding into her every thought. Was it true what Evelyn hinted at—that she, Charlotte Ginsberg, could be his Secret Santa? Charlotte couldn't contain her excitement at the thought!

Finally, Monday arrived. And though, as everyone knows, most Monday mornings are accompanied by a serious case of the blahs, this particular Monday was "blah"-free.

As you all most certainly must know by now, Charlotte was prone to daydreaming, drama, and fantasy. So, of course, she already had this most important day planned in her head. Charlotte would wear her favorite outfit especially for the Secret Santa party—a brightly flowered Marc Jacobs minidress and shiny black flats. She would

Charlotte's ready to PAR-TAY

MaRc Jacobs' MiNi (Natch) ←

brush her hair one hundred strokes and even dab on some of Emma's favorite French perfume. Mrs. Moss would have PHC (that's Pimped Her Classroom) especially for the occasion. The dim lights (dimmers to tone down the classroom's garish fluorescents or, better yet, perhaps lamps for that

romantic glow) would emphasize the glossy luster of her hair. Perhaps William would be wearing the indigo sweater that brought out the deep green of his eyes. A small box wrapped in shiny gold paper and tied with a red velvet bow would be sitting on her desk (let's insert a spotlight on the package, just for effect). The card attached would say something like, "To my Juliet, with great affection, from William" (okay, so maybe that's taking it a bit far, but this is Charlotte's daydream, and she's allowed to be a wee heavy on the cheese factor). Then, Evelyn would open Charlotte's gift and squeal with delight. "Just what I've always wanted!" she'd say. "Charlotte, how do you do it? How do you manage to always find the perfect thing, win over William's heart, and look so rockin'?"

Charlotte would simply shrug her shoulders, put her hands on her hips, and say, "Oh, it was nothing."

Back to reality, though, it was a gray Monday, as gray as London usually is in December. Charlotte and the rest of the English Roses had walked to school as usual, regaling one another with the latest fashion tips, celebrity gossip, and school news. Binah had baked Christmas cookies for the party, and Grace's mom had made her very special brown-

oh that was NOTHING!

Binah and GRace BROUGHT stuff like this

ies. There was a palpable excitement in the air as the girls walked up the lane to Hampstead School.

Mrs. Moss wasn't wearing an especially festive outfit, but she did have a wreath broach pinned to her gray pin-striped blazer and had even brought a few poinsettias to decorate the classroom. Amy, head of the Decorations Committee, had strung red and green paper streamers from the ceiling, and Binah and Grace set their treats upon a table filled with pastries and biscuits and candy. (The lights, sorry to say, hadn't been dimmed. But you didn't really expect that, did you? As if!)

Amy's Decorations →

Unfortunately, Old Mossy gave a pop quiz in math (Nicole was the only person who had studied, of course) and insisted on lecturing for a full hour on the parts of the cell before she would allow the class to exchange their Secret Santa gifts.

When zero hour finally arrived, Harold Fieldbinder passed out the packages. Charlotte sat up straight in her chair but couldn't help jiggling her leg with excitement as Harold finally plopped a lumpy package on her desk.

Charlotte faces Evelyn Eaves.

"All right, now that everyone has their gifts, you may open them," Mrs. Moss said with a smile.

Charlotte, ever the dainty lady, gingerly tore at the wrapping. And nothing could have prepared her for what was inside.

Inside the wrapping was a hand-knit green wool hat. A folded piece of paper read: To Charlotte. Happy Holidays to the queen of the theater! From, Jeanette.

Jeanette? Jeanette? What about, what about . . .

"Hey, thanks William!" Abby Weatherby held up a pretty china teapot. "I love tea!"

Charlotte's eyes stung with tears. She knew she shouldn't be so upset, but why had Evelyn made her think that William had bought her a gift? She felt like a giant balloon that had just popped. Deflated and defeated.

Just then, Charlotte felt a familiar poke in her back.

"Charlie!" William hissed. "*Pssst!* What did you get?"

Charlotte remained steadfastly focused ahead. She didn't even want to look at her four best friends. How stupid she felt! How silly! She wanted to run out of school and never look back.

Evelyn Eaves strode over and beamed at Charlotte. "Char-baby, thank you so much! What an amazing pendant!" She fingered the delicate gold chain hanging about her neck, which perfectly complemented her shiny, chestnut hair.

She looked down at the wool hat still sitting in a lump on Charlotte's desk. "What on earth is that?"

"Um, it's a hat," Charlotte replied flatly. Her stomach was turning somersaults. What would Evelyn think of her now?

to Charlotte
Happy Holidays
to the oven at the
theatre from Jeanne

EE

"Uh, *duh*! It looks like something my brother would have worn—when he was three. *Quel* tacky! Who gave you this? Toss it in the rubbish bin, where it belongs."

Charlotte's cheeks burned. What was she supposed to say?

Not so still life: hat headed for RUBBISH - BIN

She managed a weak nod, and tried to smile. And then, to her horror, Charlotte felt someone watching her from across the room. She looked up and saw that that someone was Jeanette, who had witnessed their entire conversation! Her face was wet with tears. Before Charlotte could say anything, Jeanette ran over, snatched her gift from Charlotte's desk, and fled the room.

"Jeanette? Jeanette, wait!" Charlotte called after her.

But it was too late. Jeanette was gone.

CHAPTER 8

Make Friends, Not Enemies

i have an idea!

At lunchtime, Charlotte didn't much feel like eating the tuna tartare Nigella had packed for her. In fact, her stomach felt as if it was tied into several double knots. Nothing had ever made her feel so despicable as the wounded look on Jeanette's face. To think that she,

Charlotte Ginsberg, had caused that look was almost too much to bear.

The English Roses rallied around their friend.

"Charlotte, it's okay," Binah said, giving her a squeeze.

"It wasn't your fault, Charlie," Grace pointed out. "That nasty Evelyn trapped you!"

"But it must have looked like I agreed with her!" Charlotte burst out as tears pricked her eyes. "I feel like a horrible person. And Jeanette was never anything but nice to me!"

"So why didn't you say something, Charlie?" Amy asked. "If you know Evelyn's a total phony, why did you keep quiet? And why did you get her that expensive gift?"

"B-b-because she's so . . . " Charlotte searched for

the right word. "Perfect!" she said finally. "She's so popular, and all the boys run after her, and maybe it's silly, but all of that makes me want her to like me."

"There's nothing wrong with wanting people to like you," Nicole said. "But you don't need a classy piece of bling to do it. And you don't need to put others down to do it."

"She's right," Grace agreed. "Evelyn should like you for the same reason we like you—just 'cause you're Charlie!"

"And Jeanette worked hard on that hat," Binah added. "I saw her knitting it during recess."

Charlotte nodded, then sighed, wiping her eyes. "Okay. So I messed up. How can I make things right with Jeanette?"

"I have an idea," Amy said, with a gleam in her eye.

join us
as we
set the
stage
for a
great
Holiday
Celebration...

CHAPTER 9

Kindness Counts

"Hey Evelyn, can I talk to you for a sec?" Charlotte asked, approaching the lunch table.

Evelyn was lunching with her usual gaggle of fawning admirers. A perky smile lit up her face. "Of course, Char! Sit right here! I was just showing Ricky and Sue and Abby the absolutely divine necklace you gave me."

"Well, that's what I wanted to talk to you about," Charlotte began. "The thing is, I think what you did to Jeanette is really, really awful. In fact, I think it stinks!"

"I'm sorry—what did you say?" Evelyn asked incredulously. A hush fell over the cafeteria, and Charlotte felt her cheeks burn with shame, but then she looked back at the English Roses, who were all smiles. Grace nodded encouragingly.

"You know exactly what I'm talking about," Charlotte continued, her voice picking up confidence. "You just can't treat people that way."

"Charlotte, this really isn't the time," Evelyn snapped.

"Maybe not, but I don't really care. You don't deserve that necklace. I wish I had never given you such a lovely gift."

"Get real!" Evelyn smirked.

"I'm totally real." Charlotte smiled sweetly. "*You're* the phony."

"Fine," Evelyn snarled through clenched teeth. "I don't want your lame necklace anyway." She took it off and threw it at Charlotte, then turned back to her friends. "I think we're done here."

Charlotte's head was throbbing. Everyone in the cafeteria seemed to be staring her way.

Now she just had to find Jeanette.

The Gift of Friendship

Charlotte finally found Jeanette hidden in the ladies' loo (which, every Brit knows, means "bathroom"). Charlotte heard sniffling coming from one of the stalls and peered underneath to find Jeanette's feet sticking out.

She lightly tapped on the door. "Jeanette? It's Charlotte. Are you okay?"

"What do you want?" Jeanette sniffed brusquely.

"To say I'm sorry," Charlotte replied. "To say that I love your gift. It was so sweet and thoughtful. I . . . I shouldn't have let Evelyn put words in my mouth like that."

"But it was what you were really thinking," Jeanette accused angrily from behind her hiding place in the stall.

"Not at all!" Charlotte countered. "I was a little surprised, because Evelyn made me think that William was my Secret Santa, so I was expecting something from him. But I love what you gave me. It's just . . . it's simply . . ." she searched for the right word. "Perfect," she finished.

"Really?" Jeanette's voice sounded hopeful.

"Swear on my shoes," Charlotte promised. "Now, would you please come out of that silly stall, because there is something I need to give you!"

There was a click as the door unlatched, and Jeanette slowly came shuffling out, her face puffy from crying. She peered into the mirror. "Ugh! I look like a . . . a dead rodent."

Charlotte giggled. She couldn't help it! Which made Jeanette start giggling. Soon the two girls were practically rolling on the floor, holding their bellies, tears rolling down their cheeks. Charlotte noted that it was a good thing she was already in the loo, as she felt she might pee her pants!

When they had recovered, Charlotte held out the necklace. "Here. This is for you," she said. "You deserve it."

Jeanette was wide-eyed with astonishment. "But . . . but Charlotte! Isn't this what you gave Evelyn?"

Charlotte waved her hand in the air. "I told her off, and she gave it back. It looks much better on you, anyway," she said. "Here, let me help you." She leaned over and fastened the clasp. "Perfect!"

"Wow," Jeanette said. "It's so beautiful. Charlotte, thank you!" And at that moment, Charlotte knew the meaning of the phrase "giving is receiving." For the joyful look on Jeanette's face was a gift enough for three Christmases and Hanukkahs put together!

"I was thinking," Charlotte began, "that you and I should start Hampstead's first official drama club."

Jeanette's grin widened, until it seemed to light up her whole face. "Really?!"

"Well, after winter break." Charlotte winked. "I think we've both had enough drama to last us the month of December."

And with that, the two girls linked arms and walked back to class.

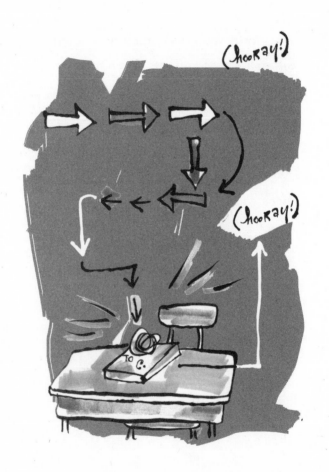

CHAPTER II

Some Dreams Do Come True!

ut Secret Santa didn't seem to be over yet, as there was a small package wrapped in shiny silver paper sitting on Charlotte's desk when she returned.

What on Earth could this be? she wondered, tearing off the silver wrapping. Inside was a CD. "Dear Charlie, These songs made me think of you. You obviously need some of my amazing musical taste in your life. Happy holidays. From, William."

Charlotte's heart skipped a beat as she looked at the handmade CD case, which was plastered with magazine cutouts. So, he wasn't exactly Shakespeare when it came to romantic sentiments. Charlotte definitely didn't mind.

She turned around to thank William, who was pretending to work hard on a math assignment. "Hey, William. Thanks for the CD. It's really cool."

He glanced up sheepishly. Though he would never admit it, Charlotte could tell he was blushing a bit. I mean, it was windy and cold that day, but still. . . .

"No problem, Charlie," he said casually, running a hand through his hair. "Happy Secret Santa Day."

Charlotte looked at her best friends, who were grinning at her, then winked at him. She put on Jeanette's knit hat and smiled at William.

"Yeah, it *is* a happy Secret Santa Day."

The End

MADONNA RITCHIE was born in Bay City, Michigan, and now lives in London and Los Angeles with her husband, movie director Guy Ritchie, and her children, Lola, Rocco, and David. She has recorded 18 albums and appeared in 18 movies. This is the seventh in her series of chapter books. She has also written six picture books for children, starting with the international bestseller *The English Roses*, which was released in 40 languages and more than 100 countries.

JEFFREY FULVIMARI was born in Akron, Ohio. He started coloring when he was two, and has never stopped. Soon after graduating from The Cooper Union in New York City, he began drawing for magazines and television commercials around the globe. He currently lives in a log cabin in upstate New York, and is happiest when surrounded by stacks of paper and magic markers.